THIS BLOOMSBURY BOOK

BELONGS TO

....

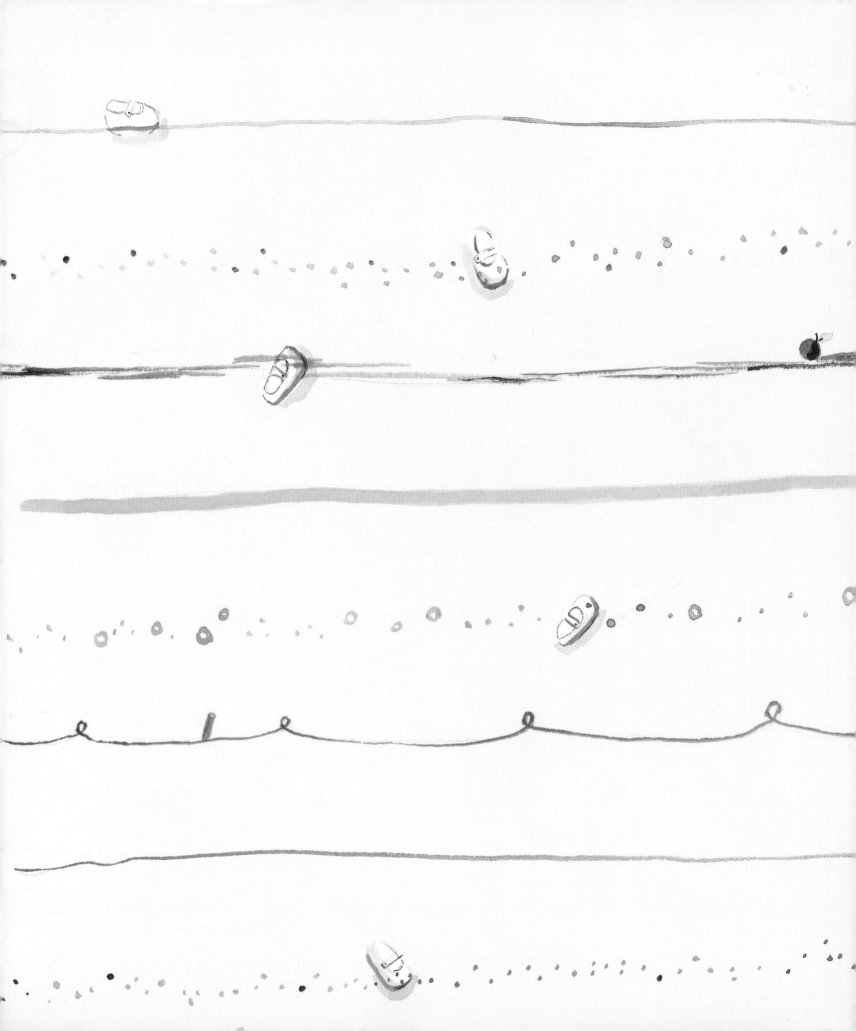

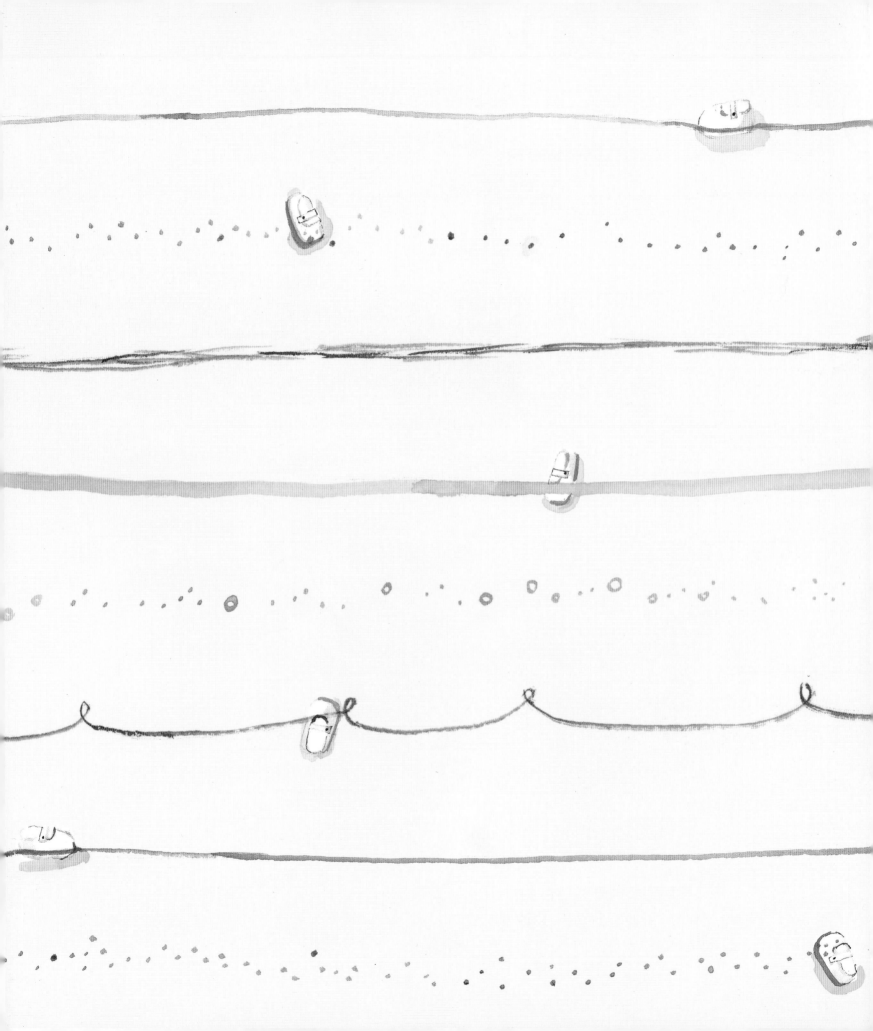

For Cliff, with all my love – D.S.

To my little bump – H.N.

First published in Great Britain in 2006 by Bloomsbury Publishing Plc
36 Soho Square, London, W1D 3QY

First published in the United States in 2006 by Bloomsbury Publishing

Text copyright © Dashka Slater 2006
Illustrations copyright © Hiroe Nakata 2006
The moral rights of the author and illustrator have been asserted

A CIP catalogue record of this book is available from the British Library

ISBN 0 7475 8206 8

9780747582069

Printed in China

1 3 5 7 9 10 8 6 4 2

All papers used by Bloomsbury Publishing are natural, recyclable products made
from wood grown in well-managed forests. The manufacturing processes conform
to the environmental regulations of the country of origin.

Baby's New Shoes

by **Dashka Slater**

pictures by **Hiroe Nakata**

BLOOMSBURY
CHILDREN'S
BOOKS

Baby's got some brand-new shoes,
shiny white, with a stripe of blue.
He passed over all the rest,
chose the ones he liked the best.

White shoes.
High-jumping,
fast-running,
fine-looking
shoes!

Mama and Baby take a walk.
Baby brings some coloured chalk.

Uses red to draw a rose

and some red loops on the toes

of those white,
high-jumping,
fast-running,
loop-de-looping
shoes!

Baby says, "Uh - oh!"

Mama says, "Oh, no!"

But those shoes just go, go, go.

Baby likes to run so fast,
spins in circles on the grass.
After all those jumps and hops . . .

...guess what's got green polka dots?

Those white,
high-jumping,
fast-running,
dizzy-spinning
shoes!

Baby says,

"Uh - oh!"

Mama says,

"Oh, no!"

But those shoes just go, go, go.

From the big tree dropping down,
plums go SPLAT and hit the ground.
Baby stops to take a peek . . .

...gives those shoes a purple streak.
Those white,
high-jumping,
fast-running,
fruit-kicking
shoes!

Baby says, "Uh - oh!"

Mama says,

"Oh, no!"

But those shoes just go, go, go.

Busy workmen making signs,
paint the road with yellow lines.
Baby hops across the street . . .

...gets some yellow on the feet
of those white,
high-jumping, fast-running,
can't-miss-'em **shoes!**

Baby says,
"Uh-oh!"

Mama says,
"Oh, no!"

But those shoes just go, go, go.

Baby finds a puddle deep,
takes a bouncing, hopping leap.
After splashing round and round . . .

. . . Baby's shoes have rings of brown.

Those white,
high-jumping,
fast-running,
splish-splashing
shoes!

Baby says, "Uh - oh!"

Mama says, "Oh, no!"

But those shoes just go, go, go.

Baby's got some brand-new shoes,
coloured bright in many hues.
Doesn't matter **what** you say —
Baby likes them best this way.

Those
speckled, spotted,
polka-dotted,
puddle-stomping,
rainbow-romping,

go-go-going shoes.

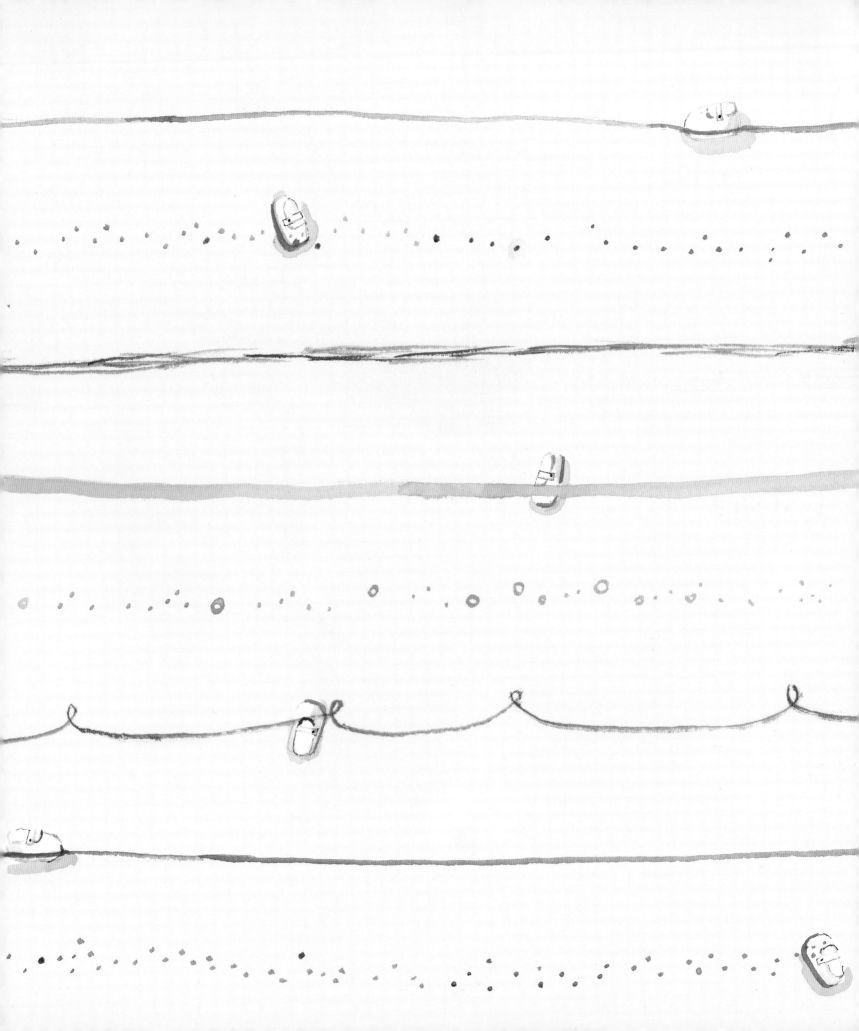

Enjoy more great picture books from Bloomsbury Children's Books . . .

Tea with Bea
Louis Baum and Georgie Birkett

Kidogo
Anik McGrory

Clementine and Mungo
Sarah Dyer

Beep, Beep, Let's Go!
Eleanor Taylor